THIS WALKER BOOK BELONGS TO:

_____

_____

_____

Text copyright © 2002 by Vivian French
Illustrations copyright © 2002 by Dana Kubick

First U.S. paperback edition 2005

The Library of Congress has cataloged the
hardcover edition as follows:

French, Vivian.
A present for Mom / Vivian French ;
illustrated by Dana Kubick. — 1st U.S. ed.
p.   cm.
Summary: Stanley has trouble deciding what to give
his mother for Mother's Day.
ISBN 0-7636-1587-0 (hardcover)
[1. Mother's Day —Fiction. 2. Gifts —Fiction.
3. Cats —Fiction.] I. Kubick, Dana, ill. II. Title.
PZ7.F88917 Pr 2002
[E] —dc21   2001035470

ISBN 0-7636-2692-9 (paperback)

10 9 8 7 6 5 4 3 2 1

Printed in China

This book was typeset in Minion.
The illustrations were done in watercolor,
gouache, and pencil.

Candlewick Press
2067 Massachusetts Avenue
Cambridge, Massachusetts 02140

visit us at www.candlewick.com

A Present for Mom

Vivian French

illustrated by
Dana Kubick

CANDLEWICK PRESS
CAMBRIDGE, MASSACHUSETTS

Mom,
Queenie,
Rex
and
ME

It was the day before
Mother's Day.
Stanley went to see
his big brother, Rex.

"What are you giving
Mom?" he asked.
"Flowers," said Rex.
"She likes flowers."

"Good idea,"
said Stanley,
and he hurried
off to the
garden.

Good idea

Stanley picked   five of the biggest

flowers

that he could see ...

but by the time
he got back inside,
all the petals
had fallen off.
"Oh, no," said
Stanley, and his
ears drooped.

-Oh, no

Stanley went to find
his big sister, Queenie.
She was counting the
money in her bank.
"Is that for Mom's
present?" Stanley asked.
"Yes," said Queenie.
"I'm giving her
a box of candy."

"Oh," said Stanley,
and he rushed
off to find his
own bank.

~Oh!

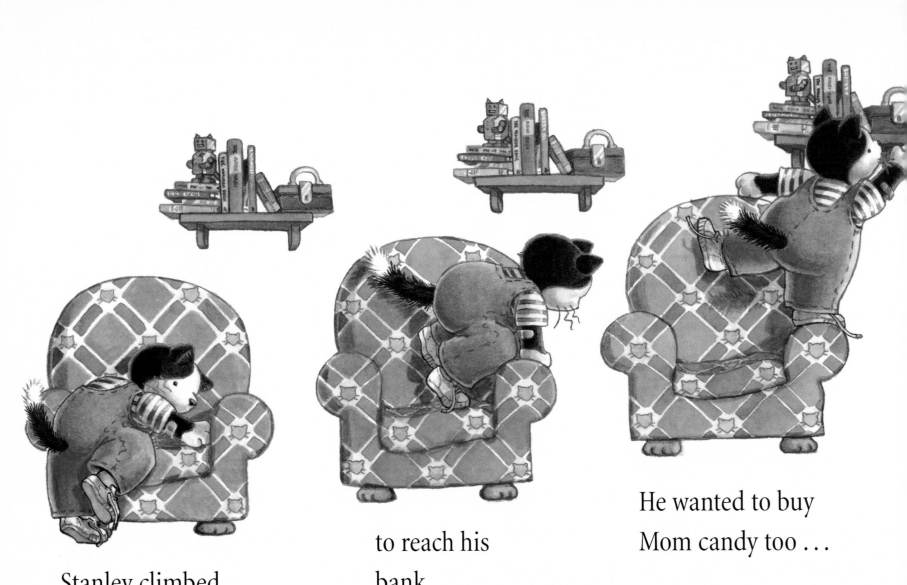

Stanley climbed
up to the shelf …

to reach his
bank.

He wanted to buy
Mom candy too …

but when the bank
fell open . . .

it was empty
except for one piece of
a jigsaw puzzle.
"Oh, no," said Stanley,
and his whiskers
quivered.

Stanley went to look for
his biggest sister, Flora.
"What are you doing?"
he asked.
"Making Mom a Mother's
Day cake," Flora said.

"Hooray!" said
Stanley, and he
dashed out of
the kitchen.

Stanley's mud cake looked

beautiful —

Oh, no

but not for long.
"Oh, no," said
Stanley, and
his tail dragged
behind him.

Stanley went slowly
upstairs to look for
a present for Mom.
He tipped out his
cardboard box of cars,
but they were all
chipped or dented.
Flora appeared in the
doorway. "Mom says
it's bedtime," she said.

That night, Stanley
didn't sleep very well.

Early next morning, Flora,
Queenie, and Rex came into
Stanley's room.
"What's the matter?" Rex asked.
"I don't have anything for
Mom," said Stanley.
"Just give her a kiss,"
said Flora. "That's
what she'd
like best."

Stanley sat bolt upright.

"I know!" he said.

"I know what to do."

"Are you coming?" said Queenie.

"In a minute," Stanley said.

Flora, Queenie, and Rex
went downstairs to give
Mom their presents.

"Flowers!" said Mom.
"They're lovely! And my
favorite candies! And
WHAT a beautiful cake!
But where's Stanley?"

Suddenly . . .

Stanley was standing
in the doorway,
carrying his big
cardboard box.
"HAPPY MOTHER'S
DAY!" he said.

Mom opened
the box.
"Stanley!" said Rex and
Flora and Queenie.
"There's nothing inside!"

To Mom

"Yes, there is!" said Stanley.
"It's a box of kisses!
    And I filled it right up
    to the top!"

"Oh, Stanley," said Mom, "it's
    a wonderful present," and
    she kissed Stanley's nose.

"Don't use them up all at
    once," said Rex.

Mom smiled. "I think boxes
    of kisses last forever
    and ever," she said.

"Yes," said Stanley. "Forever and ever and EVER." But he gave Mom another kiss — just in case.

To Mom

VIVIAN FRENCH has written many acclaimed books for children, including *The Thistle Princess,* illustrated by Elizabeth Harbour, and *I Love You, Grandpa,* a companion book to *A Present for Mom.* She says, "Dana has drawn Stanley to look exactly like my cat, Louis. But he talks and thinks like my daughter Nancy. She's the youngest of four, just like Stanley, and she says it doesn't make life easy!"

DANA KUBICK has designed everything from teapots to tin boxes, and her work has been widely exhibited. She is the illustrator of Vivian French's *I Love You, Grandpa,* as well as *Something's Coming!* by Richard Edwards. She says, "I fell in love with Stanley and nearly expected him to appear around the corner of my drawing table. My friends would ask after him as if he were the newest member of our family. I think, in a way, he is."